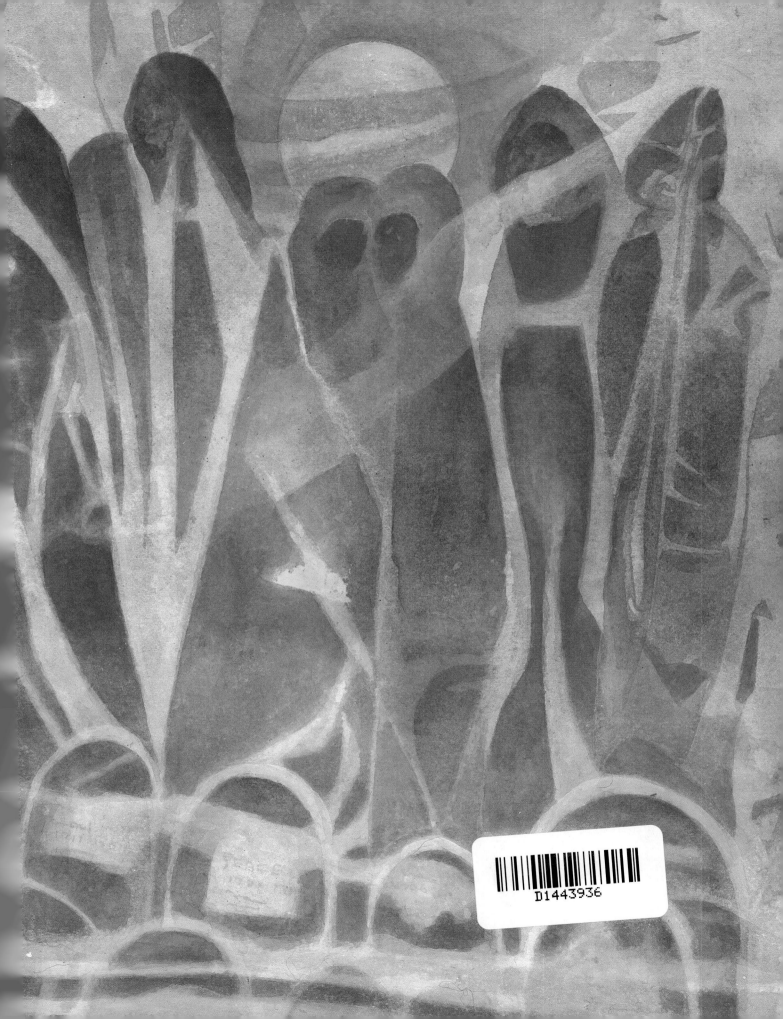

INTO THE
PUMPKIN

LINDA FRANKLIN

Schiffer Publishing Ltd

4880 Lower Valley Road • Atglen, PA 19310

Schiffer Books are available at special discounts for bulk purchases for sales promotions or premiums. Special editions, including personalized covers, corporate imprints, and excerpts can be created in large quantities for special needs. For more information contact the publisher:

Published by Schiffer Publishing, Ltd.
4880 Lower Valley Road
Atglen, PA 19310
Phone: (610) 593-1777; Fax: (610) 593-2002
E-mail: Info@schifferbooks.com

For the largest selection of fine reference books on this and related subjects,
please visit our website at **www.schifferbooks.com**
We are always looking for people to write books on new and related subjects.
If you have an idea for a book, please contact us at proposals@schifferbooks.com

This book may be purchased from the publisher.
Please try your bookstore first.
You may write for a free catalog.

In Europe, Schiffer books are distributed by
Bushwood Books
6 Marksbury Ave.
Kew Gardens
Surrey TW9 4JF England
Phone: 44 (0) 20 8392 8585; Fax: 44 (0) 20 8392 9876
E-mail: info@bushwoodbooks.co.uk
Website: www.bushwoodbooks.co.uk

WHOEVER YOU ARE,
NO MATTER WHAT AGE,
DON'T BE AFRAID TO
TURN THE NEXT PAGE.

A PEEK THROUGH THE PUMPKIN;
It's HALLOWEEN NIGHT.

SO HOP ON MY BROOM,
AND LET'S TAKE A FLIGHT.

THE BAT
WINGS ARE
FLAPPING,
THE PARTY'S
TONIGHT.

THEY SWOOP
IN AND OUT
AND MOVE
OUT OF
SIGHT.

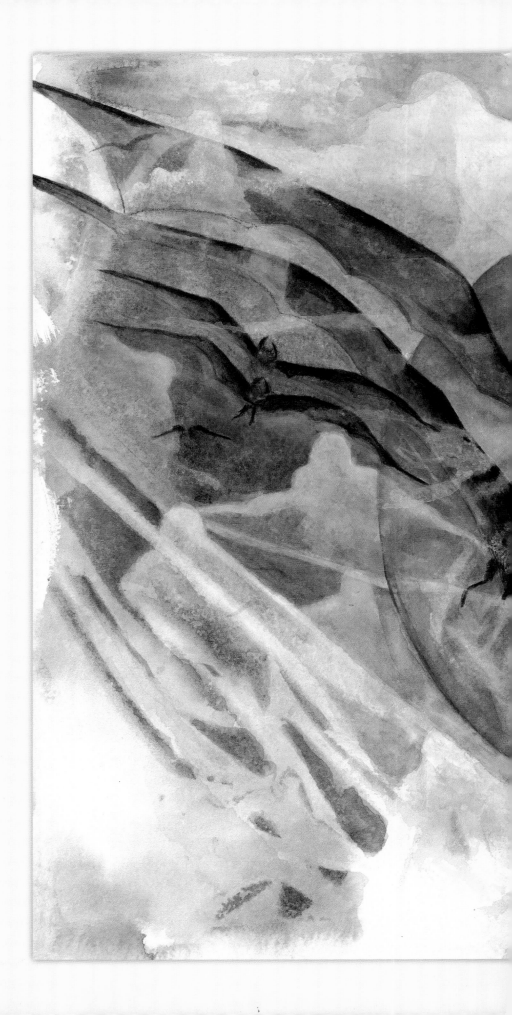

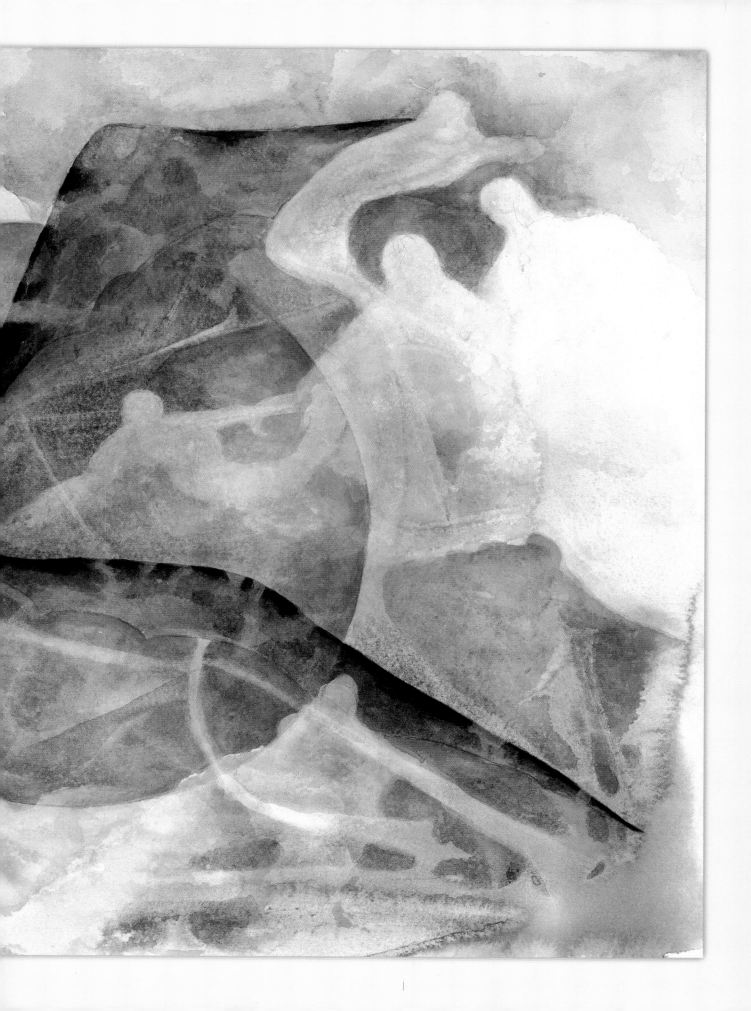

THE GHOULS
ARE ALL
OUT
TO SET
UP THE
MEETING,

TO SHARE
THEIR IDEAS
FOR TRICK
AND FOR
TREATING.

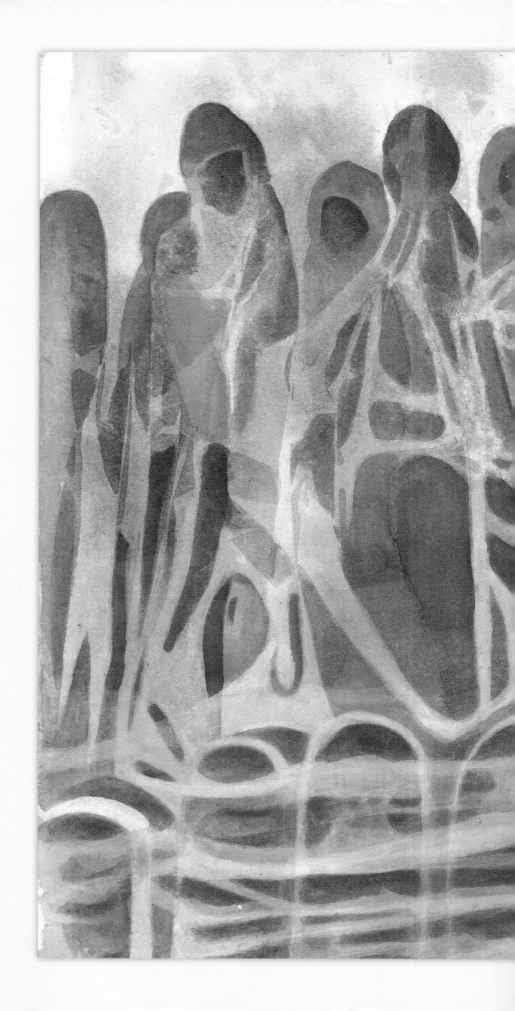

IT'S EIGHT LEGS PAST TEN,
INVITATIONS TO SEND.

THE SPIDER'S ON WEBSITES
TO SEE WHO ATTENDS.

THE WHIRL OF THE WITCH,
WITH WHIMSICAL FLIGHT,

IS MAILING OUT INVITES
OF SPOOKY DELIGHTS.

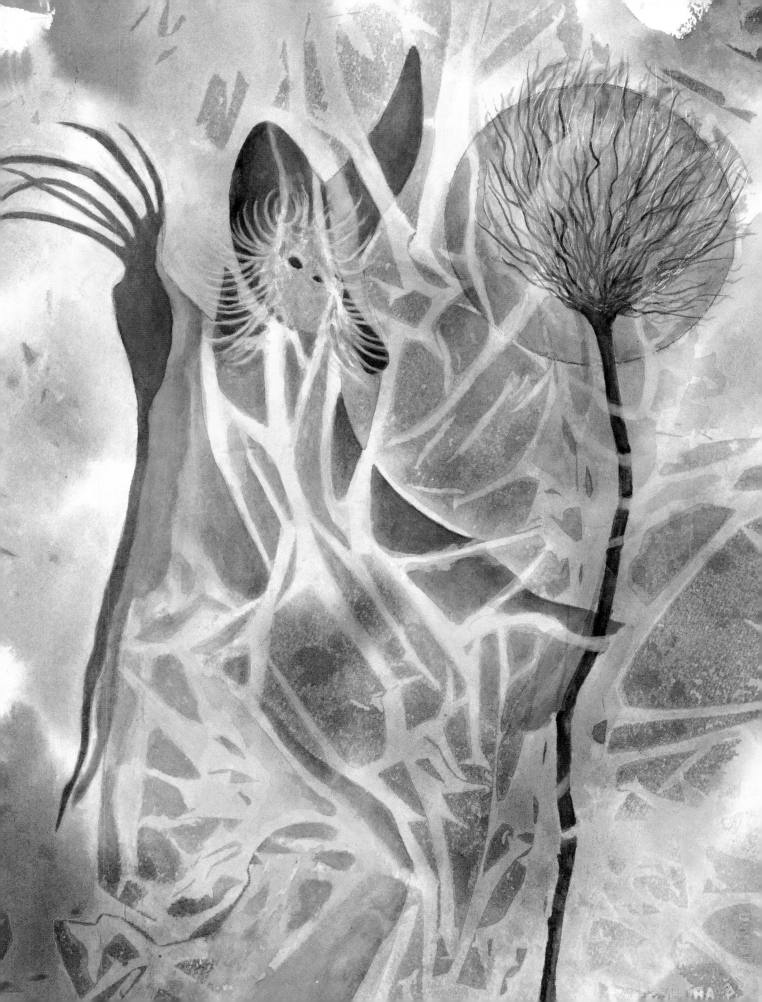

THE BLACK CAT SITS STILL,
AND LOOKS FOR HIS PREY.

BUT ALL HE CAN THINK OF
IS HALLOWEEN DAY.

They all have their jobs,
From morning to night.

Some bring out the scarecrows
And put them in sight.

The scarecrow comes out,
The proudest of all,

Will stand as the host
Of the Halloween ball.

So many
pumpkins
plan
afternoon
tea.

Their faces
are carved
for judges
to see.

WHERE SHALL THE PARTY
TAKE PLACE FOR THE NIGHT?
IN A SPOOKY OLD CASTLE
WITH GHOSTS ALL IN SIGHT.

THE HOUSE IS NOW HAUNTED,
FOUR FLOORS FULL OF FUN.
IT'S CREEPY IT'S SPOOKY
AND VERY WELL RUN.

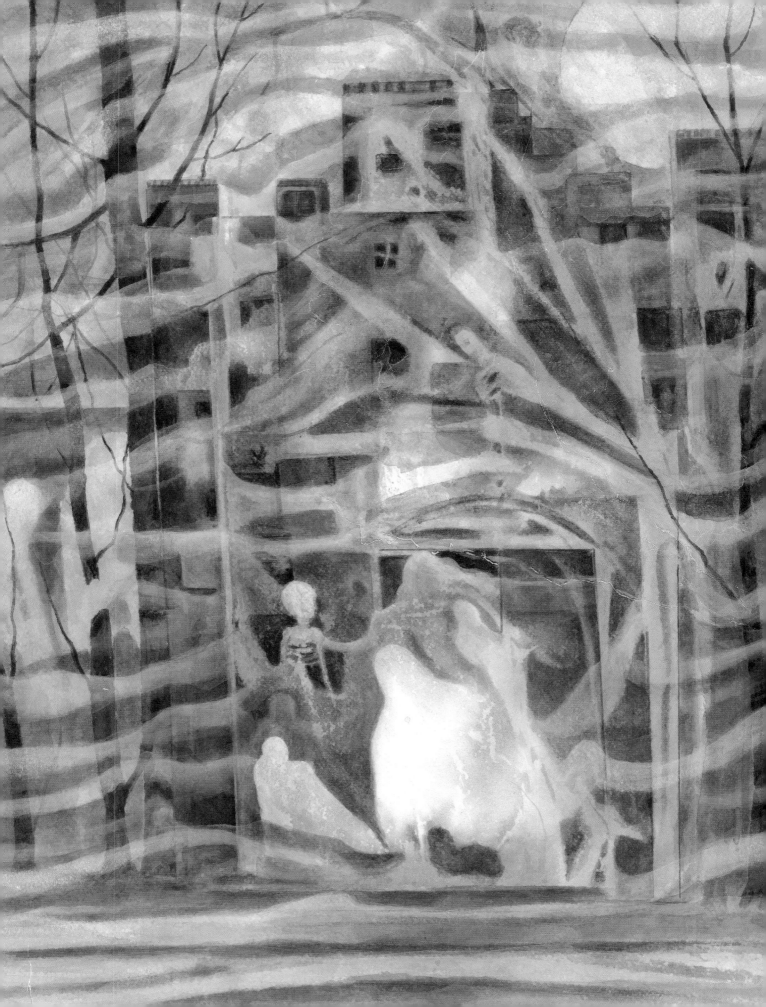

THE
GRAVEYARD,
HOW EERIE.
FOG COVERS
THE GATE.

AND ALL
NOW WHO
ENTER,
MAY RISK
THEIR OWN
FATE.

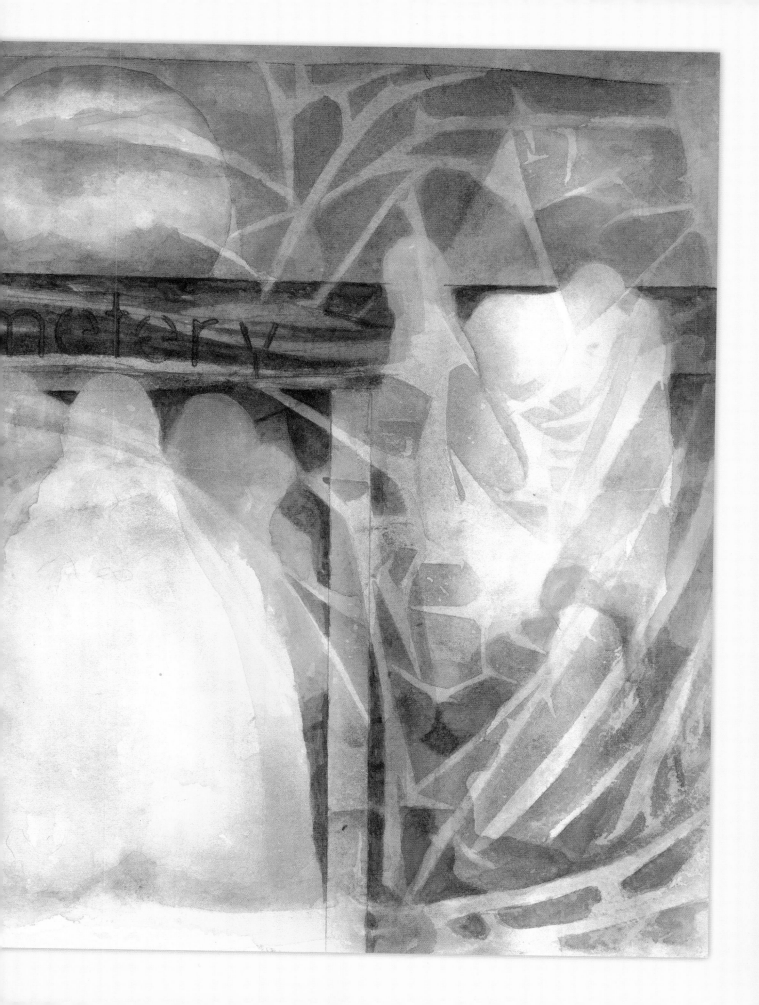

THE
PARTY HAS
STARTED.
THE GAMES
WILL BEGIN.

IT'S
HALLOWEEN
NIGHT,
WITH PRIZES
TO WIN.

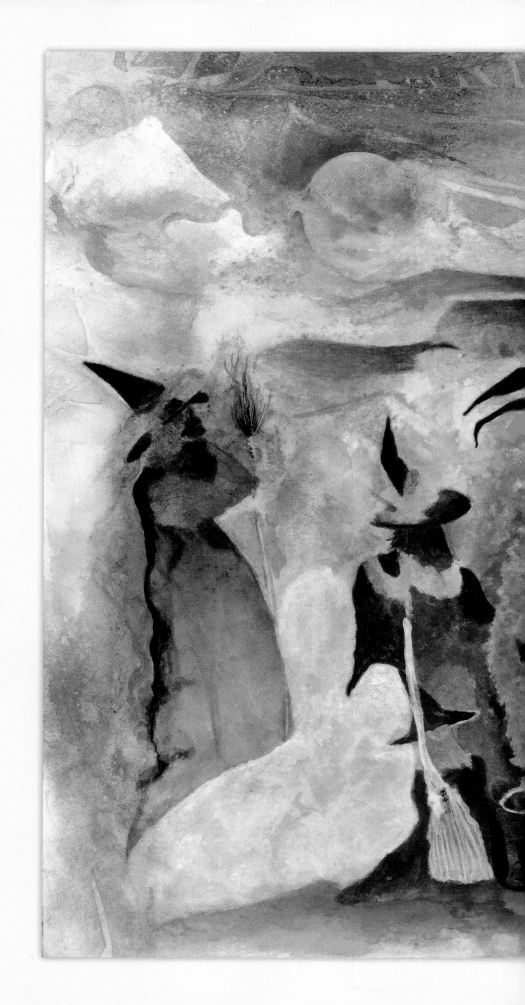

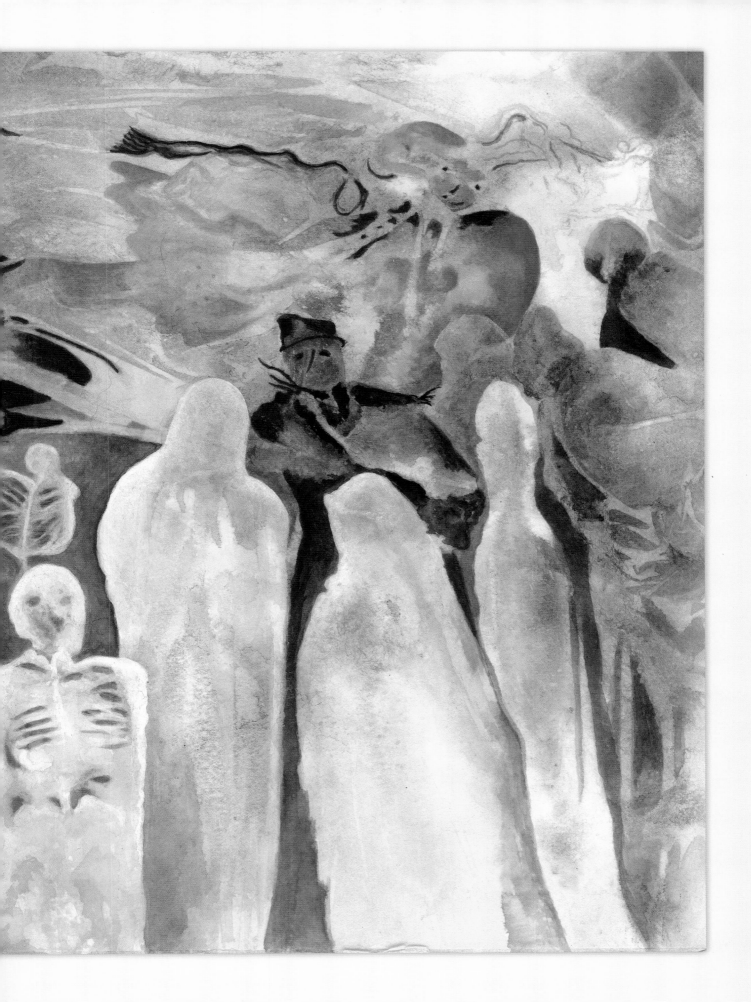

THE CAULDRON IS BUBBLING
WITH THE OLD WITCH'S BREW.

A DASH OF HER SPELL
WILL MAKE IT A STEW.

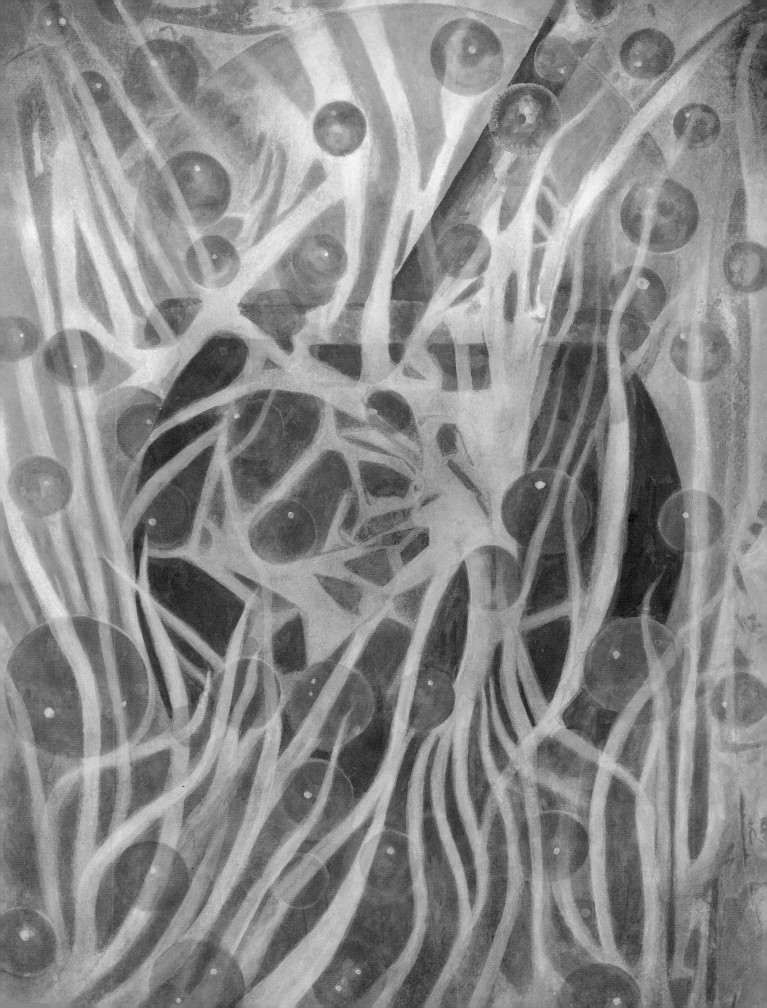

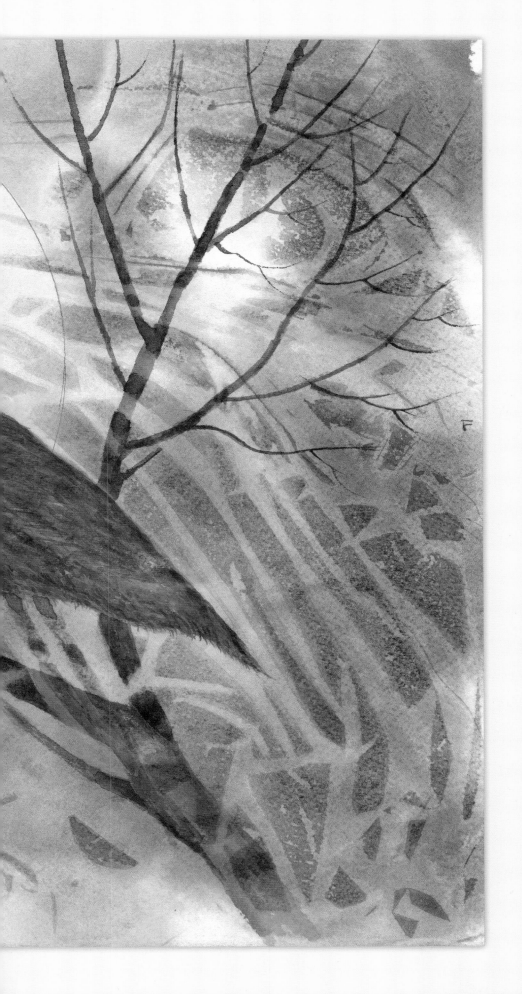

THE RAVEN
THAT SITS,
AND SINGS
OUT OF
TUNE,
CROWS
NIGHT SONGS
TO ALL
BY THE
FULL OF THE
MOON.

THE SKELETON DANCE
WILL BE A DELIGHT.

THEY'LL JIG TO THE LEFT
AND JIG TO THE RIGHT.

The ghosts
all hold
hands,
Around
they do go.

Their
choice of
this dance
May win
best in
show.

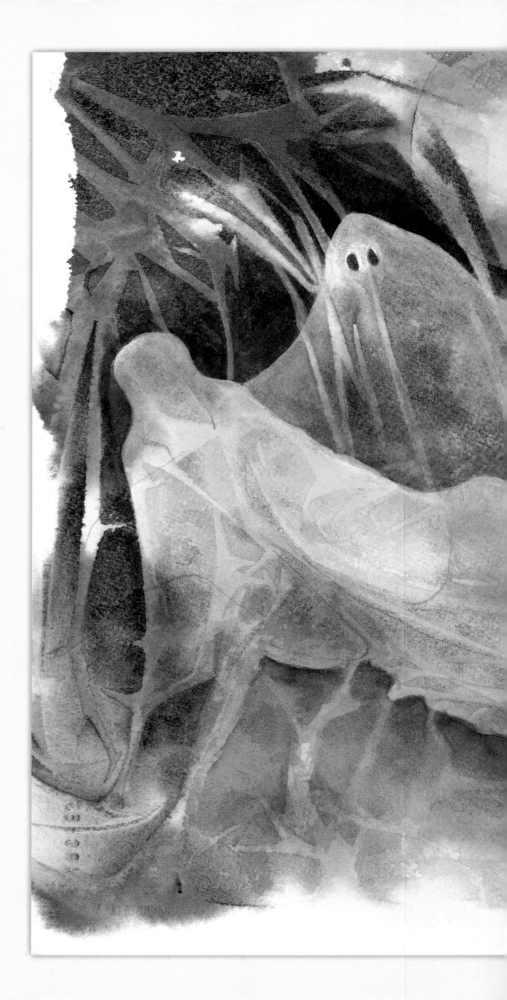

THE PUMPKIN MAN FLIES
WITH UTTER DELIGHT.

HE JUST WON FIRST PLACE.
THE PICK OF THE NIGHT.

THE GHOSTS ARE ALL FLYING
AND TURNING AROUND.

THEY'RE GETTING SO DIZZY,
THEY CAN'T TOUCH THE GROUND.

THE GHOSTS
ARE ALL
TRYING
TO REACH
FOR THE
MOON.

THEY KEEP
CHANGING
COLORS,
FROM
MORNING TO
NOON.

GATHERED
TOGETHER,
AT LAST
THEY HAVE
COME,

TO HONOR
PAST SOULS
WITH
AWARDS
FOR SOME.

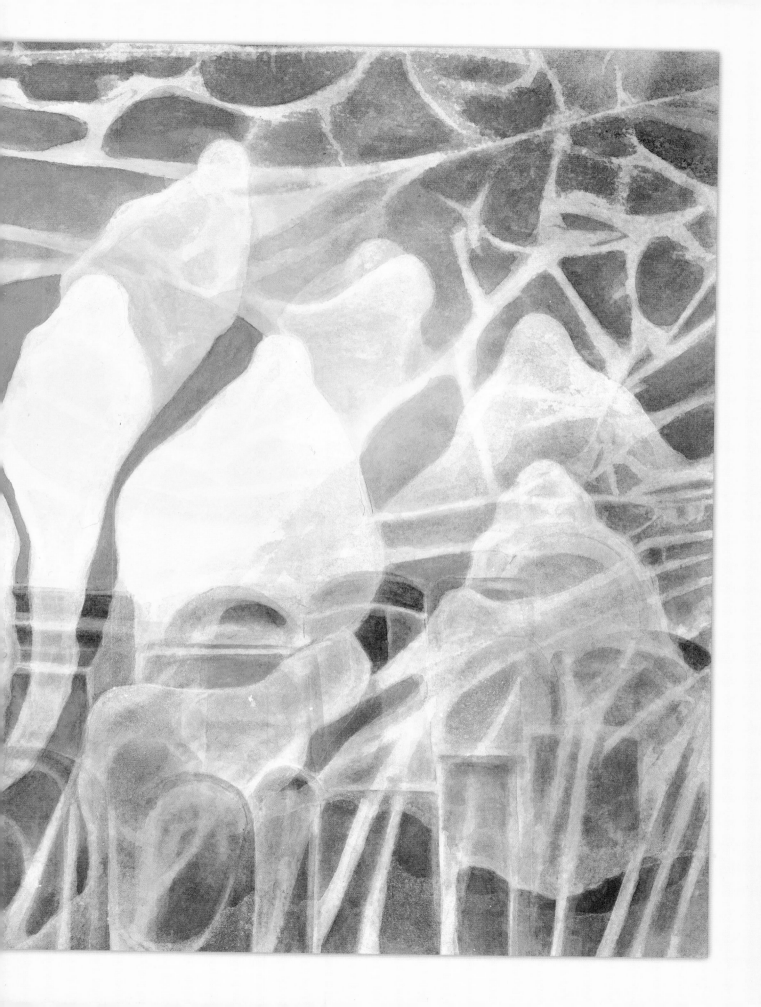

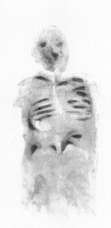

THE RAVEN TAKES FLIGHT
IN SEARCH OF HIS NEST.

HE SANG ALL HIS SONGS
AND NOW NEEDS A REST.

FLY BACK THROUGH THE PUMPKIN,
AT HOME YOU WILL BE.

MAY YOU ALWAYS REMEMBER
YOUR JOURNEY WITH ME.

HERE ARE SOME OF THE PASSENGERS,
ON THIS PAGE YOU NOW SEE,

WHO HAVE TAKEN THIS JOURNEY
AND RIDE WITH ME.

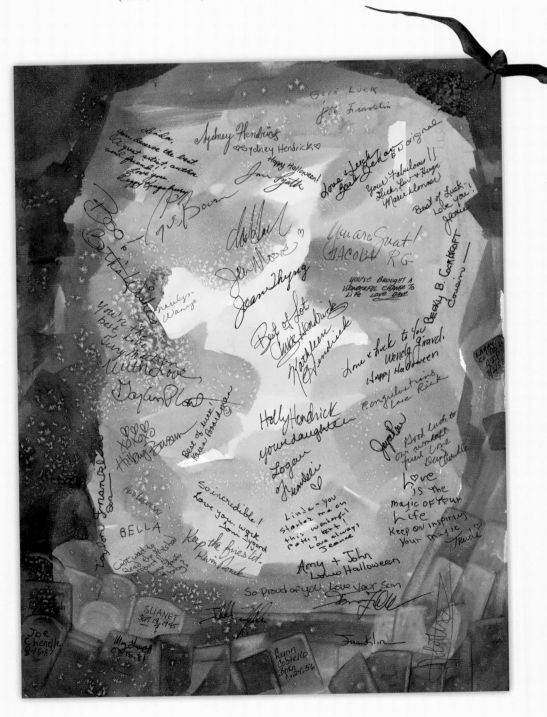